This book belongs to:

p r o j i t

ISBN 978-1-84135-193-3

Published by Award Publications Limited,
The Old Riding School, The Welbeck Estate,
Worksop, Nottinghamshire, S80 3LR

www.awardpublications.co.uk

13 4

Printed in Malaysia

Award Young Readers

The Gingerbread Man

Author

Rewritten by Jackie Andrews

Illustrated by Terry Burton

AWARD PUBLICATIONS LIMITED

Once upon a time, a little old man and a little old woman lived together in a little old house in the country.

Their children were all grown up and the little old man and the little old woman were lonely. So one day while she was baking, the old woman decided to make a little gingerbread man.

She rolled out the dough and cut it into the shape of a little gingerbread man.

She gave him currants for eyes, raisins for buttons, and some red sugar for a mouth.

Then she called the little old man to see what a sweet little fellow the gingerbread man would be, and she put the pan into the oven to bake.

Some time later when she thought the gingerbread man was done, she opened the oven and took out the gingerbread man.

With a bump and a jump, the gingerbread man leaped to the floor. Out of the house he ran, calling back over his shoulder, "Run, run, as fast as you can. You can't catch me, I'm a gingerbread man."

The little old man and the little old woman ran out of the house and down the road after him, but they couldn't catch the gingerbread man.

Soon he met a cat and the cat said, "Not so fast, little gingerbread man. I want to eat you."

The little gingerbread man ran on and, as he ran, he called back over his shoulder, "Run, run, as fast as you can. You can't catch me, I'm a gingerbread man." And the cat could not catch him!

So the little gingerbread man ran on until
he met a dog and the dog said, "Not so fast, little
gingerbread man! I want to eat you!"

But the little gingerbread man only ran faster, and as he ran he called out, "I've run away from a little old woman and a little old man, a cat, and I can run away from you too, that I can!"

He skipped merrily along singing, "Run, run, as fast as you can. You can't catch me, I'm a gingerbread man!"

So he ran on and they all ran after him down the road, but they could not catch him.

By and by the gingerbread man met a cow in a field, and the cow said, "Not so fast, gingerbread man! I want to eat you."

But the little gingerbread man only ran faster, and as he ran he called out, "I've run away from a little old woman and a little old man, a cat, a dog and I can run away from you too, that I can!"

And he skipped merrily down the road singing, "Run, run, as fast as you can. You can't catch me, I'm a gingerbread man!"

So he ran on and they all ran after him, but they could not catch him. By and by he met a pig and the pig said, "Stop, gingerbread man. I want to eat you!"

The gingerbread man ran on, and as he ran he called back over his shoulder, "I've run away from a little old woman and a little old man, a cat, a dog, a cow, and I can run away from you too, that I can!"

And he skipped merrily down the road singing, "Run, run as fast as you can. You can't catch me, I'm a gingerbread man!"

So he ran on and they
all ran after him, but they
could not catch him.

Presently, however, the little old man and the little old woman stopped, for they were completely out of breath and could not go a single step further.

Then the cat stopped, and the dog stopped, and the cow stopped, and they all watched while the little gingerbread man and the pig ran merrily along. But soon even the pig had to stop for a rest.

After a while the little gingerbread man passed a fox sitting on a tree-stump and he called out, "Run, run, as fast as you can, you can't catch me, I'm a gingerbread man."

The fox only laughed, so the little gingerbread man sang out over his shoulder, "I've run away from a little old woman, and a little old man, a cat, a dog, a cow, and a pig, and I can run away from you too, that I can!"

The fox got up from the tree-stump and he said, "But I don't want to catch you, so why do you run away from me?"

The little gingerbread man stopped running and the fox said, "Well, as long as we are going down the same road, don't you think we might as well walk along together?"

So they went on and on and after a while they came to the bank of a very wide stream.

The little gingerbread man looked this way and he looked that way, but there was no bridge across the stream.

"Just jump on my back," said the fox. "And I will help you across the stream."

So the little gingerbread man jumped on the fox's back and the fox started to swim across the water. After a while the stream got deeper, and the fox said, "Get up on my shoulders, little gingerbread man, or you will get all wet and melt away."

Once more the water got deeper and the fox said, "Now get up on my head, gingerbread man."

So the gingerbread man got up on the fox's head.

Snap! went the fox, and the gingerbread man was half gone.

Snap! went the fox again, and the gingerbread man was all gone!

But that was all right – gingerbread men are made to be eaten, and the little old woman made another one the very next day!